# You're the Real Hero

## Operation Call-Time Courage

Featuring DJ
A Hero Kids Club Story

Written by: Melvina A. Smith
Illustrations: Nabil

 Published by: The Mel Perspective Press Imprint and Brand: Hero Kids Club | You're the Real Hero Series Printed in: United States of America First Edition: 2026

Disclaimer: This story is inspired by the experiences of military families. Names, settings, and details may be fictionalized to protect privacy. This book is not affiliated

with or endorsed by the U.S. Department of Defense or any military installation.

LLCN: 2026903340

DJ stared at the clock. Tick... tock... tick... tock... Tonight was call time. DJ's heart felt jumpy, like popcorn. He really, really missed his parent.

Trent burst in holding a toy phone.
"Riiing riiing!" he shouted.
DJ laughed, then sighed.
"Not yet," DJ said.
Trent whispered, "Waiting is the hardest mission."

DJ had so many things to say. He wanted to tell about school. He wanted to tell about the Glow Dance. He wanted to tell about April being kind. And there was one more thing... a secret smile in his heart.

DJ went to his room and looked at his cowboy.
He whispered, “what if I forget my words?”
His cowboy coach sat tall.
DJ nodded.
“Okay. I need a plan.”

DJ walked to the door and took a deep breath. "DJ lined up his dinosaur squad like brave guards by the door." He lined them up extra straight. "Guard my brave," DJ whispered. Trent peeked in and saluted. "On duty!"

His mom called out, "Hero Kids, time for the Call-Time Plan!"
DJ blinked. "We have a call plan?"
Trent shouted, "We have ALL the plans!"
His mother smiled and held up a card.
It said: OPERATION CALL-TIME COURAGE

Step one said: Write it down.
DJ grabbed a paper and a crayon.
He drew pictures so he wouldn't forget.
A book, a glow bracelet, a soccer ball.
And a small drawing of April with bright sneakers.
DJ whispered, "She's my friend."

Step two said: Make a Tell-You-Later envelope. DJ made the envelope. Trent added a dinosaur sticker to the front."A brave dino," Trent declared.DJ smiled.He wrote: FOR MY HERO.The envelope felt like courage he could hold.

Step three said: Practice your calm.
DJ took three slow breaths.
In... out... in... out... in... out...
The parent whispered, “Your voice matters.”
DJ nodded. “Even if it’s quiet.”

Step four said: Choose a buddy.
DJ chose… his mom.
Trent chose… everyone.
"I'm everybody's buddy!" Trent said.
DJ laughed. "That's true."

They set up the call spot. A chair, a blanket, and a tiny dino on the table. DJ placed his cowboy nearby too.
“Cowboy courage,” DJ whispered.
Trent whispered, “Dino courage too.”

The phone buzzed once.
DJ froze.
Then it buzzed again.
DJ's heart raced fast-fast-fast.
His mom said, "It's time."

Although DJ felt anxious, excitement bubbled up inside him as he prepared to share all his great news with his dad.

DJ's mouth opened, then closed. All his words tried to hide.
His father on the screen said, "It's okay. Take your time."
DJ did Dino Breath. Big in… slow out…
Then DJ whispered, "I missed you."
DJ pulled out his drawings.

DJ pulled out his drawings.
He showed the glow bracelet.
He showed school.
He showed a ball.
Then he held up the picture of April.
DJ's cheeks warmed.
He said softly, "April is my friend.
She checks on me."

His father smiled.
"I'm glad you have a kind friend," he said.
DJ nodded.
He whispered, "Sometimes I want to tell you everything right away."
His father smiled and said, "And you can. One brave sentence at a time."

Trent leaned in close to the screen.
"Are you coming home soon?" he asked.
His father shared, "As soon as my mission is complete."
DJ squeezed his tiny dino.
He remembered: Love stays close, even far away.

The call started to get fuzzy.
The picture froze.
DJ's stomach dropped.
His father reassured him, "That happens sometimes. It's not your fault."
DJ took a breath.
His father's voice came back for a second:
"I love you. I'm proud of you." The call ended.
DJ held the envelope to his chest.

The call ended.
DJ held the envelope to his chest.
His mom said, "You did it."
DJ nodded.
"My words came out," he whispered.
Trent said, "Your brave was loud!"

DJ walked to his door.
He lined up his dinosaur squad again.
This time, he added one dino holding the envelope.
"Good job, team," DJ whispered.
His cowboy watched like a proud friend.

At bedtime, DJ clicked on his night light.
He took three calm breaths.
He whispered the words that helped his heart:
"Night light on, brave heart strong."
Trent called from his room, "Goodnight, Call-Time Hero!"
DJ smiled. "Goodnight."

**His mother tucked him in and said the words DJ loved most.**
**"DJ, you're the real hero."**
**DJ smiled and whispered back,**
**"Even when I have lots of words... and they come out one brave sentence at time."**
**Mission complete.**

**Operation Call-Time Courage (for readers)**
**When you're waiting for a call, try this:**

1) Draw your words, so you don't forget.
2) Make a Tell-You-Later Envelope.
3) Take three calm breaths.
4) Say one brave sentence at a time.

**Remember: Love reaches you, even far away.**

www.ingramcontent.com/pod-product-compliance
Lightning Source LLC
Chambersburg PA
CBHW042143030726
47599CB00002B/599
* 9 7 8 1 9 6 9 9 7 1 1 1 2 *